1

Finding Shelter from the Cold

An Ice Age Tale of Wolves and Man

Nathaniel Robert Winters

ISBN9781453710401

This book is dedicated to three dogs that have been among my greatest companions in my lifetime, Ripple, Autumn and Coco. I am thankful that some of their early ancestors found shelter from the cold.

FINDING SHELTER FROM THE COLD

An Ice Age Tale of Wolves and Man

Prologue

The wolf glided quickly across the field. She had picked out her prey, a large deer with huge antlers. The pack looked to her for guidance. She was the alpha-bitch, second in command. The buck was in rut and had just lost a battle to another male for sexual dominance.

It was cold, Ice Age cold, and the wolf had a thick coat of winter white fur.

Frozen tundra met the forest. The deer's head bobbed up and down as his antlers scraped against the frozen tree bark. Foam dripped from the buck's mouth and steam rose from his nostrils. He was powerful but exhausted in defeat, vulnerable.

The wolf started the attack, chasing the reindeer. Yet even in exhaustion the deer was quick. Seeing his growling attacker, he bounded off, outracing the sprinting wolf. The prey ran for the open space away from the trees, putting fifty yards between himself and his attacker. The buck relaxed, feeling safe when the next wolf jumped out. A male leader of the pack had been hiding in plain sight, lying flat against the icy tundra. These canine hunters chased their prey as a pack, in tandem, taking turns to exhaust the deer.

There were five in the pack, a male with a black spot on his muzzle and four females, including the alpha-bitch with a brown spot on her tail. Mostly the wolves were all snowy white.

They exhausted the vanquished buck and he turned to face his attackers. The full pack surrounded their prey. The buck still formidable, his antlers and head bent low ready to charge, but out of breath. The wolves took turns attacking his hind hamstrings. Helpless, the poor creature turned in circles trying to fend them off, his very life at stake. All five canines bore into him, biting at his legs, his throat, tearing the deer's flesh with powerful jaws and sharp teeth.

Soon the wolves' coats were bathed in blood and no longer white. Covered in red, they ripped into chunks of meat. The pack won this Ice Age battle of life and death but things can change quickly.

Halfway finished with their meal, twilight descended, sending a glow into the western sky. A loud roar stopped them in mid-bite. The wolves looked up to see the two huge white arctic lions approaching. The large cats wanted the kill. As formidable as a pack of wolves could be, they were no match for the lions. The male wolf growled, teeth flashing. He tried to defend the carcass, not giving ground fast enough. The first large lion swiped with deadly claws, catching the lone wolf along his right side, leaving a huge gash. The wolf's blood mixed with the deer's on his coat and he retreated, mortally wounded. As the sky darkened and night descended, the young wolf lay dying.

Chapter 1

The Wolf's Story

I held my tail high because I'm the alpha-bitch, proud. I have earned my position by guile, guts and glory. The other female wolves do not have what it takes to be leader. I plan the hunts, find shelter and lead the pack. The male is the absolute leader, but I do most of the real work.

Now the pack looked to me since our leader was down. How stupid to challenge a lion, though males tended to be that way, not knowing when to retreat, when to give up the fight. He lay dying in the snow, whimpering, my lover, my friend, our leader. Six eyes looked at me to lead them.

What to do? I nuzzled my fallen mate. He groaned. I licked his face and turned. With a nod to the rest of the pack, we left. A wounded wolf brings all types of predators.

Temperatures were falling. I could smell snow in the air, and we needed shelter from the storm. We headed to a small cave that we had dug under a rock last summer in the cool mud. It was a few miles away and it was time to go home. We jogged to the cave, our bellies half full but our hearts empty. We crawled under our rock and lay tightly together to share our body heat against the wicked night's cold. Exhausted, we fell into a restless sleep, knowing our pack must change.

The morning dawned colder and wetter. Snow had fallen during the night and crunched under my paws. I liked to walk alone at times, to get away from the others and think.

As clouds hung in the sky I walked to the ridge top to watch the two-legged wolves. They didn't have fur, but wore skin from animals on their backs. They lived in huts during the summer on the ice. I could see the wood and stretched hide that made their shelters.

I called them two-legged wolves because they were smart like us. Like wolves they hunt in packs, taking turns chasing their prey or laying in ambush like we would. But on their paws they had these long digits. They held tools to hunt; long sticks with points or weighted sticks with stones. They needed these tools because they couldn't run fast and their teeth were pathetic.

Gray Ears, another wolf, followed my scent to the ridge. She was the smallest of the pack so her tail was always down between her hind legs. She came to me and rolled on her back offering her belly in submission. I licked her on the mouth in greeting.

Gray Ears rose up with a look on her face that asked "What are you doing?"

I nodded toward the human huts. She shrugged her shoulders. She didn't understand my fascination with the humans but, somehow, I knew humans and wolves were linked.

Chapter 2

Orick's Story

My people call me Orick. At five foot five inches, I've grown to be the biggest man of my tribe. I am told I've lived seventeen years. I remember fifteen of the cool Ice Age summers when the reindeer came in numbers too many to count. The migration always brings plant-eating beasts to the growing grasses of the tundra. Summer does not last long and we hunt constantly to store enough food to last the long winter.

My tribe elected me chief. We are twenty-four: eight men, ten women and four children. My little son Jurick toddles around, learning to walk. Silvana, my beautiful wife, never lets him out of her sight, because dangerous predators could nab him in an instant. My mother Noana also keeps watch over Jurick, but she is old, probably over thirty summers.

In the coldest part of the winter, we live in a cave away from the icy winds. Eight months later we emerge like a butterfly from a cocoon to put up our huts and hunt the reindeer. The sun climbs each day, almost at its highest level. The ice is melting and water levels are rising. The fish almost jump onto our hooks. We hang fish to dry for the long winter.

I saw the wolf on the ridge watching me as I walked away from the village. Wolves are dangerous but I was safe with my wood spear and stone ax. I have seen this female before, the one with the spot on her tail. I studied her with curiosity. Wolves are smart like people. Like us, they hunt together taking turns chasing their prey or lay in ambush, camouflaged by their white coats on the frozen tundra.

I walked closer to the wolf. She did not move away but watched me with a new alertness. When I got within about thirty feet, she let out a low growl. I took a small piece of dried meat from my pouch and put it down in the fresh snow, retreated about twenty feet.

The she-wolf approached slowly and gave me a quick growl, as if telling me to stay back. She smelled the meat and grabbed it quickly, retreating up the hill where she gulped it down. After the snack, the wolf squatted and peed on many spots on the hill. I watched these animals enough to know she was marking her territory.

The wolf's behavior suddenly changed. She turned away from me and the fur on her back stood up. She showed her teeth and growled. I heard and smelled the enormous furry mammal before I saw him.

A young rogue bull mammoth had come over the hill about one hundred and fifty yards from me. Male mammoths can be very dangerous. They don't eat meat, but young bulls can be very nasty. I have heard stories about them attacking lions and bears for the fun of it.

My spear and ax felt suddenly insignificant in my hands. The pachyderm came closer and bellowed loudly through his trunk and stomped his front legs. I stood confused. If I ran he probably would run me down. If I stood my ground he could easily stomp me. I was terrified, temporarily frozen. As the mammoth approached me, the she-wolf ran up and growled. Turning his tusks towards her instead of me, I watched in shock as the mammoth chased her. With amazing ease, she dodged the big animal leading him away. I was left alone, shocked. For some unknown reason, the wolf had saved my life.

Chapter 3

The Wolf's Story

I cannot explain my actions. Instinct took over. Maybe it was because he gave me meat as if he were part of the pack. Man is slow and I am quicker. I saw no danger in the awkward mammoth. He chased me for two hundred yards. I changed course so he could not follow my quick moves. The frustrated beast stopped and bellowed a terrific blast through his trunk. He stomped off, no doubt to cause some other mischief. I have seen a bull mammoth uproot trees for no apparent reason.

I returned to our pack by following their scent. They were not far from our small rock cave. Gray Ears came to me, and I nuzzled her flank. There were only four of us left, too small a pack to bring down a great deer. We needed to increase our numbers and join another pack. There were other wolves to the north and the south. I smelled their marked territory. I decided to lead our pack to the north. That group had only six wolves, but including us, ten would be too large a group to feed and we could be rejected. But another reason drove me towards the new pack. I knew I was pregnant and I would need the protection of a big pack to defend my pups.

The scent told us we had crossed the boundary and were on foreign and dangerous ground. We spotted the northern pack just after noon. It was cloudy, and a haze hung over the frosty ground as we approached. The alpha male, a very large wolf, approached me like a lynx stalking prey. He growled and showed his teeth. I bowed in submission.

He jumped at me and howled loudly, growling more. He came over and sniffed, recognizing my scent from his southern border. The male wolf seized my throat, growling and taking total control, holding me down for a full minute. When he let me up, he mounted me to show total dominance. Tail held high, he went to a rock and urinated, leaving his masculine scent. The alpha male was no real threat to me. He was just putting on a show. The wolf that worried me was the alpha bitch.

There were four females in this group, one young male and the lead male. When the alpha she-wolf approached, I did not back down. She stalked me slowly, growling and showing her teeth. I exposed my canines and we attacked each other. She bit at me and I grabbed mostly fur. We were going at it for a few minutes when Gray Ears came to my defense. That was a big mistake. Two females and the young male attacked Gray Ears, biting and quickly slashing her. She whimpered and retreated but the adrenaline of the pack was flowing and they kept up the attack until they had killed my friend. My two female pack survivors rolled on their back in submission. Now all the females in the pack turned toward me growling. I had no choice but to retreat. While running away, I looked back. The two young females from my pack would be safe with them but I was rejected and alone. I put my tail between my legs and trotted back to my cold, lonely rock cave.

Chapter 4

Orick's Story

Silvana, my wife, grabbed Jurick. The clear morning was warm, only one hide warm. The ice melted faster. Mud pooled with water as the temperature climbed. Grass growing on the tundra flats let us know the reindeer would soon return.

"What's wrong?" I asked Silvana.

"Get your spear," she said in a low voice.. "There is a wolf stalking outside camp."

I grabbed my spear and went to join the other men. I looked to the north end of camp and saw the spot on the tail of the wolf.

"I know this wolf!" I yelled to the others. "Let me deal with her. Keep the children away."

Everyone had heard my story of the wolf that saved me from the mammoth. We told stories around the campfires but I knew that most people did not believe my tale.

I put down my spear and slowly approached the animal. Her winter coat was shedding. I could see she was really skinny. She seemed different. The she-wolf's head was lowered and her tail was between her legs. As I came within ten yards she growled at me but did not show her teeth. I stopped and approaching her with empty hands.

"It's okay, girl. I'm not going to hurt you," I said softly.

I took out a piece of dried meat and held it out for her. Her head went up, sniffing in the air. She drooled as she came forward very slowly. When she was a few feet from me, the wolf jumped forward so quickly that I almost did not see her grab the meat from my hand. She moved back and swallowed it in one gulp.

"Stay here," I said to the wolf and

pointed with my hand. I was surprised she did.

I went back to camp, got a bowl of rabbit stew made with meat and tubers dug from the thawing ground. When I moved quickly back to the spot-tailed wolf, the others in my tribe looked at me as if I were crazy.

"Orick, how can you share our food with this *animal*?" My friend Surick asked.

I ignored him and went back to where the canine was laying on her belly with her forefeet in front of her. I moved a few feet in front of her. I knew she could smell the stew. The she-wolf actually smacked her jaws together. She did not growl this time but stood with her tail raised high. I put the bowl down in front of me and took a step back. The thin white wolf came forward and took a few licks with her long tongue. She looked up at me and turned her head sideways as if she was thinking. Rapidly, the stew was gone, swallowed in almost one gulp. She turned and walked away wagging her tail. Could I have a special bond with this dangerous animal?

Two days later, I was gathering wood late in the day for the evening cooking fires. Looking up, I glimpsed the familiar spotted tail outside of camp. A cold wind had come from the north but the wolf did not even take the precaution of coming from downwind to our village. She carried something in her mouth. I felt naked walking outside of camp without my spear, but I trusted the female wolf to do me harm. I walked to her quickly. She was about fifty yards from camp. As I advanced, she dropped the thing from her jaws and retreated a few paces away. I noticed the white long ears first. My wolf friend looked back at me. I picked up the carcass. We would have fresh rabbit in our stew tonight. As the lone wolf walked away, I thought I saw her smile.

Chapter 5

The Wolf's Story

Mice, mice and more mice, they were everywhere. When the early summer thaw comes it becomes mouse season. Where do they come from? I have no idea but they make for great eating. I have recovered from my hunger after returning to our…no, I guess it is only *my* rock cave.

While the mice satisfied my hunger, I was lonely and missed my pack. I tried to amuse myself by playing with my food. I grabbed a mouse by the tail, throwing him up in the air and gobbling him in one bite. Playing with rodents was not enough. I needed companionship. I howled at the naked sky and there was no answer. As the sun got higher and the morning fog burned off, I headed back to the man camp.

I had not been back in a few days, now that my hunger could be satisfied by mice. Orick was the only creature of his kind that I ever allowed near me. I hoped to keep it that way, Men were dangerous and unpredictable.

I approached slowly from the north as I had during my last encounter. When I got fifty yards from camp, I stopped and

32

lay on my belly, waiting. Within a few minutes, Orick came to me. I knew his scent now and could smell him even before he appeared.

"Hey, girl, I can see you are fatter. What have you been eating?" He asked.

I could not understand what he said but he talked in a very calming voice. The man held out a piece of dried meat. I took it quickly and retreated. I ripped the meat into small bits and ate it slowly, not being as hungry as our last encounter.

While everybody in the village was watching Orick and me, a lynx streaked into the village from the south and grabbed a man-child by his clothing. I knew the

men were too slow to catch such a cat.
Adrenaline pumped through my body and I
darted after the lynx. He would have been
too fast for me, but dragging the man-child
was slowing him down. I cut him off thirty
yards from the camp. The cat hissed and
swiped at me but dropped his prey when I
growled and showed my teeth. The man-
child sat in shock and looked at me. I sat
and guarded him. I sniffed his hindquarters
and recognized a scent similar to Orick's.
As the men ran up with their spears held
high, I retreated, leaving the boy unhurt.
Orick picked up the boy and held him close
to his chest. He looked over his shoulder at
me and said something I did not

understand.

He threw me another piece of dried meat and led the group back to the camp. Orick's she-wolf greeted him with water in her eyes. I sat and watched them until it got dark.

Chapter 6

Orick's Story

It was early dawn and I hated to leave my warm fur blankets to relieve myself. Before I got out of the hut I could hear them in the distance their hooves stomping. I looked out away from the forest to the knee-high grass of the tundra. In my view, there stood the hundreds of reindeer. They were back. Six men would go on the hunt. Two women would stay behind with the children to watch for predators, although most bear, lions, and of other tribes of men would be out after the reindeer as well.

Hunts were dangerous and very often not successful, but killing the reindeer meant our survival. We would use every part of the carcass – the hide for blankets, huts, and clothing, the meat for food, and the fat and bone for soup.

The six of us set out with a spear in one hand and an ax in the other. The usual plan was for two of us, Turick and me, to circle around and isolate a reindeer as we had practiced. We would then scare and chase the animal back toward two men holding a rope to trip the prey while two others waited with spears.

I looked up and saw that the she-wolf was walking twenty yards to our right. I was surprised but not shocked to see her. She had been at camp often during the past week. I had started to call her Loana. The wolf soon responded to her name and looked up when I called.

As we got close to the herd, Loana sprinted ahead. I could see she-wolf pick an older female deer and cull her from the others. On her own initiative, the wolf was acting like part of our tribe and began chasing the deer back to us.

"Run the trip line," I yelled to Purick and Yurick, two of my tribesmen.

They pulled the rope tight under the

deer's feet and down she fell in front of us. Three spears were pitched and found her flank. Deeply wounded but wide-eyed she jumped up and started to run away, but the wolf cut her off and chased her back to us. The reindeer tried to veer away but three more spears quickly found their target. Blood spurted and the deer collapsed, her front legs giving way. Turick and I jumped on her, and smashed her head with our axes, putting her out of her misery.

We tied the big body of the reindeer by the legs to our spears and carried our trophy home singing a victory song. The she-wolf walked close to us now. She had earned a place with her fellow hunters. And

I saw that wolf's smile on her face. As we came to camp, she stopped at the edge of the huts.

"Come, Loana." I said calmly and she followed me.

We put the carcass down and I took out my stone blade. Cutting a chunk of meat off the deer, I threw it to the wolf. She ripped at the big pieces, chewing voraciously. The women went to work on the deer's body with stone blades.

That night we gathered around the campfire and Noana, my mother, being the oldest female, led the prayer. She thanked Mother Nature for the grass that brought the reindeer. Turick, who has seen 13 summers now, had completed his first hunt that day and had earned the privilege of retelling the capture the deer. It was his first hunt story. I have heard many over my years but none had ever included a wolf hunting with our tribe. Loana, our she-wolf, curled up next to the fire, belly full and dozing. Turick's story that night become legendary.

Chapter 7

The Wolf's Story

I knew I was never really part of their pack. Hunting with the men was as natural as breathing. When the hunt was over, I stayed just outside their camp. Orick and I had a special bond. I trusted this man and knew he trusted me even with his man-child. I let him touch me and I licked his skin like I would a puppy. He tasted like his smell, not like food...comfortable. His touch felt strangely good, like the warmth of another wolf.

I did not trust the others and would growl if they came too close. I knew they didn't trust me either, especially the females around their children. I could smell their fear. So each night I retreated to my rock cave. It was cold and lonely without other wolves. I worried about my belly getting bigger. What would happen to my puppies without a pack to protect them?

Chapter 8

Orick's Story

Late summer turned colder and muddy. Loana would roll in the mud, which I believed protected her skin from the sun and camouflaged her white fur. The spotted-tailed wolf stayed apart from the tribe. If another man approached, she growled and showed her teeth. No one wanted to anger this proven killer. In spite of saving Jurick from the lynx, my people kept a wary eye on her when she was in the camp.

But when the tribe hunted, everything changed. The wolf became part of every successful hunt. We learned together, getting better with each hunt, and knowing what to expect. It was our tribe's most successful summer ever. The women stayed busy smoking meat for the long winter ahead.

Almost every day I watched her sitting outside of camp. By late July, I had touched this former wild animal, even scratched under her jaw and behind her ears. She would rub her face against my leg and lick my hand. The other men reported that she urinated around the camp, leaving her scent to ward off other wolves and rival animals. After a successful hunt, she stayed late into the evening just outside the camp to receive her reward. Usually a leg and the bone would be cut off the carcass and I would take her the meat. She always ate quickly and then would disappear over the hill with the remaining bone. In the morning she would reappear looking for me to rub her muddy belly which looked to be getting fatter each day. Unlike our tribe, she could not dry food for the winter and I assumed the big belly would help her survive.

One morning when I woke and went out to relieve myself, I noticed the reindeer were gone. The season was over. The sun was getting lower in the sky and the days were getting shorter. Winter would be upon us soon. It was time for our move. Our hide-covered huts were fine for summer but we lived in a large cave during the long cold Ice Age winter. That night we would have a feast to celebrate the end of the hunting season.

The day was spent packing. We carried our bundles on large wood hut supports, dragging the back ends on the ground and the front parts of the branches over our shoulders. The hides of the huts would be stretched between the wood supports, our bundles piled on top.

Thanks to our wolf it had been a

great hunting season and our bundles would be heavy with pounds of dried meat, roots, and other wild vegetables gathered by the women of the tribe. Mother Noana, had great knowledge of medicinal herbs and spent a good part of the summer replenishing our supply of the special plant parts, mosses and fungi. Even some dried worms are believed to be good for digestion. Personally, I don't think the worms help, but I've seen that first hand that molds and fungi heal wounds.

Just past midday, Loana appeared outside camp. I noticed she had gotten much fatter as summer wore on. I went to greet her. I reached out to her and scratched her under her chin and on behind her ears. She made a soft howl and nuzzled my left leg. Looking closely at the she-wolf, I noticed that her teats were elongated. I was shocked.

"Are you pregnant, girl?" I asked.

She looked up at me with those intelligent eyes.

"I sure wish you could talk." I said to her..

I was shocked at the thought that Loana could be pregnant. She had been so active during our hunts and I had never seen her with another wolf. I guessed that the mating took place before she came to us.

That night, we would hold a great feast, our last meal in our summer village. Reindeer steaks and ribs were grilled over a low fire basted with herbs and the juices of wild berries. Tubers were smoked for hours with small twigs and pine leaves. The women cooked all day while the men took down the huts and packed. My mouth watered as I worked. The smell in the air could attract other animals, even lions, so we kept vigilant. Most predators would not attack an armed camp of men, but you never know. The smell had one wolf smacking her lips but we weren't really worried about her.

Evening came earlier now; we were

getting close to the time when daylight is equal to darkness. Our work stopped and it was time for our feast! We gave thanks to Mother Nature by cutting a piece of meat and throwing it in a big bonfire. The fire would consume the meat and the ashes would go back to the earth. Next we cut a big rack of ribs for our canine hunting partner. She was not used to cooked meat, but it did not deter her; the wolf attacked the rack with tail wagging and growling at the meat. We laughed at her as we served ourselves.

After the meal, we acted out the hunts of the summer, as was our tradition. My wife, Silvana, played the part of the wolf. We laughed that night 'til tears ran down our cheeks. Loana curled up after circling a spot just outside camp to sleep. We slept outside because the huts were taken down and we hoped it did not rain. In the middle of the night I woke to find the she-wolf had curled up next to me.

The next morning was colder. We knew Mother Nature was telling us to go to our winter cave. Loana followed us a respectful distance behind.

It was a five-mile journey along the edge of the forest to the rocky outcropping at the base of the foothills that lead to the mountains. Not much lived above the hills since ice clung to the highlands all year long. The entrance to the cave is hard to find behind a large group of boulders. When we leave in spring we cover the small entrance with rocks and brush so other tribes won't find it. Battles have been fought by different tribes over caves. They can be the difference between life and death in the cold winter.

It looks like the rocks and brush had been disturbed and as we stood outside of the cave, Loana's nose went up and she growled loudly. The cave was about thirty feet long and ten feet wide. It had a hole near the back side that went up to the top of the hill that let in light during the day and we could use as a chimney for cooking.

There was still plenty of daylight so we knew we could see well enough inside.

"Surick and Lurick, will you take your spears and ax and enter the cave?" I asked.

The two men pounded their chests with their fists.

Surick said "It would be a privilege to be the first to go in".

We moved a few stones and brush from the entrance and the wolf growled deeply. Something was in there. The two men entered and their eyes adjusted to the dim light as they heard a load hissing and a deep growl, then a large roar. A large cave bear met them, smacking and snarling. He

waved a huge clawed paw at the two men
who held him off with their spears.

"It's a bear!" Surick yelled to the
tribe as the two retreated towards the
entrance.

Of course Loana already knew about
the bear, she could smell him. She growled
at the entrance protecting her new pack but
was not foolish enough to take on a full-
grown bear. We moved back from the cave
in case the bear came out to defend his new
home. I quickly came up with a plan.

"Gather some kindling and brush, we
will smoke him out" I said to the group.
"Keep the children back. After we throw
the smoking brush into the cave, be ready

with your spears."

Normally I would not want to face a full grown cave bear but we were a tribe of great hunters. I used my flint rock to make a spark that caught the dry brush on fire, we added kindling to build up a quick hot fire, then added leaves to make the fire a smoking mass. We used our stone axes to heave the smoking mass into the cave. Within a few minutes the angered bear came out hissing and growling. We threw our spears and hit him from all sides. The sharp points dug in past his grayish-white fur and into his body. The attack angered the bear and he pounced on the closest man to him. Surick went down but two men stabbed the bear from his flank, the sharp spears drawing more blood. The cave bear turned, confused. Blood oozed from his thick fur.

A wounded bear is a dangerous beast, but we were unafraid absorbed with our task. We didn't let up. Loana was growling at the bear, adding to his confusion. He wanted to retreat, but we didn't let him. More spears flew into his body and as he toppled, two men attacked his head with axes. He had a hard head and still didn't die. The bear struggled to his feet and came right at me, but blood obscured his eyes and I darted out of the way and threw a spear into his neck. He fell again and this time we made sure he would not get up. An ax hammered at his head, while two more spears stabbed at his neck. He rolled to the side, growled loudly and died. We would eat fresh bear meat in our cave that night.

Chapter 9

Orick's Story

Silvana was an amazing woman. A great cook, hide tanner, and she was learning about medicinal herbs from my mother. What made her unique was her art. She used charcoal to draw figures on the cave walls. She used plants to make special colors for her craft. That winter she drew pictures of the fight with the bear and even a reindeer hunt with my wolf friend.

Our cave was very crowded, just big enough to store our caches of food and places to sleep. A fire burned under our roof and a small hole allowed air for our fire. During the day we rolled up our blankets to give us room to move about a little, while the long cold winter began to blast outside. Loana had taken residence by the entrance where the cave was coldest, away from the main part of our tribe. I went over every day to say hello, feed her some food, and pet the now obviously pregnant wolf.

Just about the time of the fall equinox, that special sacred day, when light is equal to night, the wolf hid in a cave vent too small for a man to squeeze into and stayed without food or water for days. We

60

could hear the crying of pups. When she emerged, she had four tiny pups with her. She would only allow my family near her litter. There was one male and the other three were females, including a little runty spotted bitch. The three large pups were snow white. The little spotted pup was the friendliest and played with Jurick who walked and talked now.. We named the runt Spotana.

Jurick loved to play with the little pup while the other three growled and ignored him. While Spotana tried to play the other pups rejected her, especially the male pup. He bit her and prevented her from sucklng. Loana allowed this dominant

61

act to play out, somehow knowing the little spotted pup would have to struggle to survive in the wild.

Nine months we stayed in the cave. Silvana finished her painting and our food caches were getting very low. Joana, Surick's wife, was not as lucky as the wolf. When it was time for her to give birth, the baby would not come out. My mother tried to help giving a special herb potion and even reaching inside to help the baby find his way out but he would not come. Joana died in the morning on one of the coldest days in the winter. We took her body outside away from the cave, the icy cold driving through us as we dragged her already cold body away. There were four of us on the death party, Surick, Noana, Silvana, and me. We gathered wood in the cold and started a fire under Joana's body. As the flames grew, we said a prayer to Mother Nature. We felt Joanna give her last warmth from the glow of the flames. The group sang the song of death and when the fire grew dim, we headed back to the cave.

Chapter 10

The Wolf's Story

Winter had shouted its loudest. I
knew it was time to separate the wolf pups
from the man pack. They needed to be
wild. The pups had grown quickly and it
was time to wean them. I crept out of the
cave during the worst part of the winter to
snare a rabbit or a careless chipmunk and
bring the fresh meat back to the pups for it
was also time for the young wolves to eat
meat.

I knew the little spotted pup would

not survive in the wild. She was the last to feed on my milk and was tiny. The other pups would not let her eat the meat I brought back for them until they had their fill. Sometimes they would not let her eat at all. I was sad about this, but life is hard for a wolf. Orick's family, especially Jurick seemed to care for my smallest pup. They would give her food and the man-cub would play with her. By the end of the winter Jurick and my little spotted pup were inseparable.

The sun rose a little higher. There was a glimmer of warmth in the icy exterior. I signaled to the pups that it was time to leave the man cave. The small spotted female pup tried to go but I growled at her. She whimpered and Orick picked her up and held her fast. The four of us turned and walked out of the cave into the outside world.

It was a cold dangerous journey back to my old pack's rock cave. The three remaining pups stayed close to me. We traveled quickly, always alert and arrived after a passing of time.

Something smelled wrong at the rock cave. I knew that smell. It was a young wolverine who had taken up residence and tried to defend her new home. She posed a real danger to the young pups with her sharp teeth. I was not going to let her get a chance. As she growled and stuck out her head, the alpha-bitch came back to me. I grabbed the wolverine's head across her eyes and dragged her out. Quickly letting go of her head, I grabbed a hold of her neck in a death grip not letting the young female wolverine breathe. I held tightly until the rival predator's body went limp. Under the rock I could hear the yelps of young wolverine pups. Good, I thought. It was time for my wolf pups to learn how to kill.

Chapter 11

Orick's Story

Did Mother Nature give us the wolf pup in exchange for Joana and her baby? Spotana explored every inch of the cave and showed a healthy curiosity. Could a wolf pup live with us? I had not seen any other tribe with wolves, yet this puppy took to us like family, especially Jurick, her play partner. He would throw her an old bone and chase her to get it back. After a few minutes he would quit chasing the young wolf and she would stop running away and bring him back the bone. She would sit and whimper waiting for him to throw the bone again. The young boy would laugh out loud and hurl the bone across the cave barely missing someone's head. The cave was filled with Jurick's laughter and Spotana's yelping.

Just days past the spring equinox, the worst of the winter's wrath was behind us. It was time to leave the cave and set up camp. These were the desperate days. Our stores of food were running low and while it was warming, Mother Nature could still have very cold breath.

We left at dawn. The tribe would have to make it to camp and set up the huts before the cold evening gave way to the icy night. Since we had little food, we had less to carry which made our way a little easier.

It was a good time for rabbits in the lower hills. The ice had melted just enough for the long-eared mammals to dig roots. Many predators would attack the rabbits, but they were usually safe from us. We could not run fast enough to catch them and a fleeing bunny was almost impossible to hit with our spears. If we were settled at camp we could catch a rabbit with a snare. Even young boys learned to do that. But we were on the move, with no time to set snares.

It happened in just a split second. Spotana circled around a hare and chased it right at us; the long-eared creature almost ran through my legs, too fast for me to react. Would the young wolf do it again? Its hunting instinct was strong and soon another rabbit was heading my way. This time I was ready and I hit him with my spear, not quite killing the hare but the little wolf grabbed the wounded animal by the neck and shook him until he stopped squirming. He delivered its lifeless carcass to the feet of Jurick, as if he were fetching the bone when they played.

More rabbits came our way before we made it to the campsite. Maybe times before the return of the reindeer herd would not be so desperate after all.

Chapter 12

The Wolf's Story

I heard the howl coming from just over the ridge. It was a male wolf howl. I lifted my nose to the air but I could not smell him. We had huddled in our rock cave and caught many rabbits to survive. Soon it would be the time of mice and it was getting slightly warmer, the ice on the ground was getting thinner. My three young wolves followed me over the ridge. They were no longer little pups; they were growing fast. I saw the young male standing at the next small hill. I could smell him now and I approached him from downwind. I recognized his smell and howled.

He was the young male from the pack that

rejected me. His father probably made him

leave the pack now that he was becoming a

mature male. He lifted his head and howled

back.

The young male wolf approached me

quickly without threat. I showed him my

teeth and growled which told him to slow

down. He came to me in a stalking position

and again I showed him my teeth growling

softly. He stood up and closed the gap

between us in a slow walk, tail up and

wagging. The white male went behind me

and smelled my hindquarters. I sniffed him

in recognition. He slowly mounted me, not

for mating, but to show dominance. I would not let him dominate so easily. I threw the young wolf off me. After a few minutes of growling and fighting I rolled over exposing my belly to him in submission. He was a young healthy male and I needed him. The five of us would be a new pack, a formidable group of hunters and I would again be the alpha-bitch.

I showed the young male our rock cave and hunting grounds. He lifted his leg to pee on every corner marking his new territory. I left him with my young offspring. I walked to the hill above the man village. I looked down and saw Orick by the fire. My young pup and Jurick were running and playing together. I smiled, howled loudly, turned and jogged back to my pack.

As we went back to the rock cave, we saw mice, lots of them. They were back. Our pack would have plenty to eat.

PART 2

Chapter 1

Jurick's Story

Night gave way to day, and the icy winters gave way to the cool, wet, muddy summers. Five years have passed since my father, Orick, became a legend by befriending the she-wolf. Her daughter, Spotana has become a great hunter with the tribe. She is also my best friend. I am still too young to go on the reindeer hunts with the men and the small spotted wolf, but I hear their adventures at the evening ceremonial campfires.

"Jurick, help bring in the carcass."

It was my father returning from a successful hunt. I ran to greet the group of men and Spotana jumped on me, knocking me down and licking my face.

"Stop it, girl. Get off me," I said, laughing to my canine friend. I rose to my knees and hugged her, scratching her fur coat. Leaving Spotana, I helped bring the deer to the women in the camp who were ready with their sharpened knives to butcher the kill. Weeks of my work went into sharpening the blades, smashing stone upon stone to make the pointed ends and scraping the edges on sandstone to make them smooth and sharp.

That night we would have another

feast. Life had become much easier for our tribe since my father adopted our first wolf. Now that Spotana had taken her place we ate better than any other tribe we knew.

We added the wolf to our Mother Nature prayer and we always gave Spotana a small piece of meat during the ceremony. The story of the day's hunt was told at dinner. As usual our four-legged friend would start the attack, this time picking a doe that had moved too far from the herd. The small spotted wolf placed herself between the female deer and her herd, growling and nipping at her hooves until she ran at the men who were lying in wait on the tundra with the trip line. It was almost too easy, as the tribes' spears

pierced the flesh of the young doe. Another

successful hunt had been completed.

Lurick, my friend, had reached the

age of thirteen summers. It was time for

him to actively join the hunt. He would

participate in the next hunt for the first

time. He had been watching for years,

learning and practicing for this special day.

My friend had worked all winter making

spears and he picked out one of his best for

this first hunt. His father had given his son

his favorite ax for the occasion. Lurick

would be given the honor of throwing the

first spear.

"Jurick, it is time for you to learn,"

my father said to me as the flames died down. "You will accompany us on the next hunt. Be ready with a small spear. As you know, you only watch."

I was so excited. My blood flowed from my head and I felt faint. I was both happy and frightened to be able to go on my first hunt.

"Yes, father," I replied, my voice cracking with the "yes," sounding like a young girl and the "father" almost sounding like a man.

I will remember the day watching my first hunt, for the rest of my life. It was a cool summer's morning and clouds blocked the sunlight, giving a glow to the eastern sky. The wind whipped making me shiver from both the cold and my excitement. I watched the proceedings from about a hundred yards away with Unrick and Surick, adults held in reserve and my body guards. The open tundra was not the safest place for a ten-year-old boy alone.

The hunt proceeded as planned. Lurick was right behind the men who held the trip rope. My father Orick stood beside him, providing him confidence and experience, at the ready if anything should go wrong. Spotana went ahead of the group and staked out the reindeer herd, an instinctive hunter, looking for the weak link. The wolf picked her prey, an older buck with a slight limp. She howled and growled at the old reindeer, moving him away from the herd and towards the hunters. The deer took off running quickly not showing the limp. Then without warning a large adult cave lion darted out after the buck from the opposite side. Lions usually like to steal prey rather than chase it, but this young female had cubs waiting back in the trees.

Spotana stopped almost in mid-stride. The lion was in charge now. Predator and prey were headed directly at our hunting party. Orick stepped in front of the boy, spear at the ready. The deer bounded to the side and the lion confused by the motion of the men in front of her, attacked. Orick's spear glanced off the big feline and before he could strike with his ax, the big cat grabbed the back of his neck in a strangle hold. The other men rushed up throwing spears and the lion quickly backed off.

Orick fell with his throat cut open. I ran quickly with my spear to where he lay dying. I looked down at my brave father. Our eyes met, he could not speak but I knew his last thoughts were that he loved me.

Chapter 2

Spotana's Story

Nature called me away from my tribe, leaving in the middle of night when Jurick was asleep and wouldn't miss me till morning. I knew where my family of wolves' rock cave was located. Their scent was strong everywhere around our village. When my tribe hunted, we would see the pack chasing reindeer. I heard the pack's howls in the night. I could even pick out the call of my mother but I never answered. I had had no direct contact with my siblings since the day my mother left me with the humans. I felt no anger at her choice. I was happy and well fed with my human family. Yet I was leaving the warmth of my home for the dangers of wild wolves. Nature called me with a silent powerful howl. It was time for me to have pups of my own.

As the morning dawned, I trotted to the top of the hill and saw my siblings. I approached the wolves from upwind and they hadn't noticed me. A howl sounded from deep in my body. The startled wild wolves looked up. The alpha-male gave a curious stare. A deep howl escaped from his throat, followed by a low growl. They closed in on me, all five including my mother, two sisters, a brother, and the unknown leader of the pack.

The handsome alpha-male approached me first. He was aware of my existence, had smelled me with the humans. Their scent was still on me and he growled at me fiercely. I rolled over in submission. He closed the gap and grabbed me by the throat, then quickly let go as he took in my musky odor. Knowing I was in heat, a smile came to the face of this powerful, pure white male.

He mounted me quickly, his powerful jaws grabbing my neck. Nature took its course. He finished quickly, dismounted and howled proudly.

The other wolves approached. My largest sister was alpha-bitch. She growled and attacked but the large male came to my rescue growling fiercely at her and putting her in her place. She reluctantly submitted. While I was in heat the male would protect me; his yearning to plant a seed was stronger than the rankings of the pack.

My mother came to greet me with curiosity. She smelled my hindquarters and I sniffed her. Time had taken its toll on this wild wolf. She walked with a slight limp and her mouth had lost some teeth. The dark spot on her tail was lighter now that the gray was mixing into her white coat.

The pack was hungry and as morning passed they howled getting ready for a hunt. I would join them, and we moved out towards the tundra and the reindeer herd. We walked single-file according to the pack ranking: the lead male followed by the alpha-bitch, with my mother in the back, followed only by her smallest offspring, me. I noticed I was the only spotted wolf, all the others were almost pure white.

My tribe of people appeared absent that morning as the pack arrived on the tundra. The reindeer took a defensive position, on high alert. The fawns moved to the inside of the herd while the large males went to the outside, their large antlers poised to do battle. My sister went ahead of the pack and howled loudly, unnerving the herd, causing confusion. Then she saw a small male with a short rack moving away from the herd. She gave chase immediately, separating him from the others. My brother joined her, nipping at the young reindeer's hind legs. My mother was next to give chase, but I could tell she was slowed by her bad leg and old bones. The young buck turned back toward her and she was too slow to move out of the way of his small rack. His left antler caught her full across her side, and down she went, a loud yelp coming from her mouth. The other wolves jumped on the deer and brought him down. My brother held his neck in a death grip and the reindeer was quickly gasping for breath. The other wolves in the pack tore chunks from his skin and the deer was quickly killed.

I watched not being part of this hunting, killing machine. I went to my mother. Blood was coming from her side but she was able to get up and I licked her wound trying to clean the injury. The other wolves snapped down big chunks of meat, barely looking at us. Mother's pain destroyed her appetite and I did not know if the pack would let me share in their kill. When all the wolves had eaten their share, I moved slowly toward the carcass, my tail between my legs. My largest sister growled at me but the alpha-male growled and let me eat. He wanted a healthy mating partner.

As we left the carcass the scavengers moved in. Large crows and other birds descended first. Foxes and other small mammals would move in quickly until just a skeleton was left.

The pack turned back towards the small rock cave. My mother moved slowly, the pain showed on her face. Her wound oozed blood and turning her white coat a shade of pink. Halfway home to the rock, she stopped and lay down. She could go no further. Each of us paid tribute, one at a time nuzzling her mouth and licking her face. We then turned and walked on. Death is nature's harsh way for wild wolves. She would not be alone for long. The

scavengers would smell her blood.

Chapter 3

Jurick's Story

Spotana returned after two weeks. Glad to see her, I gave her a big hug. She licked my face her tail wagging. Our wayward wolf appeared exhausted and hungry. When I offered her food she ate ravenously. After coming back, I noticed a change in my pet. She was less playful and more mature. I soon learned what I believed made the difference in her behavior.

A hunting party of four men came across what was left of a wolf carcass. Very little was left, only some bones and part of the tail. But on that small piece of the tail there was an unmistakable spot. Loana was gone. I wondered if in death her wolf spirit would join with my father's, together hunting reindeer.

I knew that Spotana was aware of her mother's death. I had spotted her with the wild wolves of her family even though I was downwind and she did not see me. A big male white wolf accompanied her. I knew about animal matings. Father explained it as we watched males with females in the reindeer herds. Would our wolf have puppies? Time would tell.

We were to hunt that day. The reindeer would soon migrate and hunting season would be over. We still needed more meat to dry for the winter. Assigned to watch and learn, I stood with two man who would watch over me. Spotana joined the five of us as if she had never left. When we got to the tundra, the reindeer were clearly agitated and Spotana ran out of her usual formation toward me. She had smelled something unusual. Over Northern horizon there appeared a group of woolly rhinoceros. I counted fifteen of the magnificent beasts, huge, powerful and strangely beautiful. Never had I seen anything like them before. Even the most experienced men did not hunt these monsters. Their hide made the best of blankets, but a healthy rhino was unassailable. Adults were too big and strong for our weapons. They protected their young from any flanking attack keeping then to the interior or the herd. We sometimes found rhino hides after a team of lions would leave a kill. Pairs of large lions could attack a small female rhino but not even a large pack of wolves would try and attack a healthy rhinoceros.

The reindeer moved to open a path to let the huge creatures pass. We stood transfixed watching the wondrous animals go by. The rhinos filed through the opening in the reindeer never wavering. After the great herd passed, we reorganized into

96

hunting teams quickly hoping to find stray reindeer confused by the rhino crossing.

Just then we saw her, an old sickly female rhino was moving through the reindeer. She could not keep up with the herd, which made her vulnerable but still dangerous. My elders decided to attack the massive straggler.

A healthy rhinoceros moves fast with power in a straight line but is slow to change direction. Our men believed this old female would be sluggish. Instinctively, Spotana ran right in front of the animal and howled. The old rhino stopped in her tracks, startled by the young wolf. She lowered her head and charged. As easy as chasing a bone, Spotana dodged out of the way but kept the animal's attention. The Rhino almost fell trying to turn quickly enough to follow the nimble wolf.

Seeing their chance, the men attacked from both sides. Spears had to be thrown from close up to pierce the tough hide of the woolly beast. Each man came at the animal's flank and threw their first spear. The large animal showed panic, her eyes getting large with fright. Blood spouted from her thick skin. Second spears were tossed from each side of the rhino. Confused by the teaming of the men and wolf the old giant did not know which way to turn. She decided to run away toward her herd. The men expected the retreat and readied the trip line. Four of the hunters held the rope steady. The big beast caught a front leg and toppled to the ground sending up a wave of dust. Men hurled themselves on the fallen rhino striking with heavy stone axes at her thick skull. Even I joined the bloodlust swinging as hard as I could with a weighty axe. We had her. The old beast groaned and died, her skull smashed.

The kill was an enormous prize but we could not carry the entire carcass of the rhino to our tribe. We had to dress it right there. We all worked quickly using our stone knives to cut the precious large hide from the meat. We could make many warm blankets from this rhino's woolly coat. We then cut huge hunks of meat from the dead rhinoceros. What we couldn't carry we had to leave to the scavengers. I made my way back to camp proudly covered in rhino blood. Most men go their whole life without getting the chance to kill a rhinoceros. Unbelievably this triumph was my first organized kill.

It was an amazing hunt. That night we burned a large piece of meat to thank Mother Nature for creating the fantastic woolly rhinoceros. Around the campfire, we laughed and sang well into the night. I was given the privilege of telling the story of the hunt.

Chapter 4

Spotana's Story

Orick was the alpha-male of our tribe and when he died Surick took over as leader. He did fine as head of the group but I never felt close to him like I did Orick. Jurick was a pup, a playmate. We were like equals but I grew quicker so I looked out for him like an older sister.

Just a day after the rhino kill, the reindeer were gone. A steady rain beat down sending currents of mud and water through the camp. As the rain fell, Surick put off our departure to the cave. I spent more time with Silvana, watching her with

Jurick and his younger sister Risana. Silvana became the alpha-female of the tribe after her mother-in-law had died from the cold.

When we went off to the hunt, the women spent the day gathering herbs and plants, preparing hides, smoking meat, and taking care of the children. For Silvana, this included watching the toddler Risana, seeing she did not stumble into trouble or crawl too far from the camp where an animal could attack her in a moment. When I was in camp I helped keep an eye on the young girl, feeling almost like a second mother to her.

Two more days of rain followed and

it was hard for the people to pack or do anything except avoid the rising waters and the mud. Huddled with my human family in the tent-hut we watched the water beat down outside.

While in the huts, Silvana spent a great deal of time weaving rope from leather strips. The parts of the hides not used for clothing were carefully cut with stone knives for this purpose. It was exacting and time consuming work, usually done during the long winter in the caves, but this period of unending rain gave Silvana the opportunity to work on this laborious chore.

When Risana grew restless, she

jumped on me, pulling my ears or some

other part of my body. I snapped at her,

nipping when she played too hard. Other

times I nipped at her in play. I was careful,

never broke her skin while we played.

When she got too rambunctious, like

pulling my tail, I would push her off me but

I couldn't stay angry at her. I loved the

little girl.

Chapter 5

Jurick's Story

On the third day, it got colder and the rain turned to snow. It was time for the tribe to move before everything turned to ice. We worked all morning fighting off the wet cold, taking down the huts and packing our belongings. By midday we were ready to start our trek to the cave. It was the most miserable migration I remember, torturous walking, leaning our bodies against the icy North wind. Our feet oozed in the mud mixed with wet snow. The thought of the warm fire in the cave helped me put one foot in front of the other. About at the halfway mark to the cave, Spotana stopped and growled. Her body language told me that with her sensitive sense of smell something that was amiss. Surick waved his arms and gave the silent hunting signal to stop. We waited quietly watching the snow fall, then saw the migrating mammoths coming from the North.

They were far in front of us. The huge herbivores usually marched along not bothering us. They were magnificent, even bigger than the wooly rhinoceros and just as hairy. They walked in a line one following the other. Only the mothers with calves walked in twos. In the front was a great bull, the biggest animal I had ever seen. I noticed that the men grew nervous. They put down their big bundles and took up their spears.

Surick said, "I don't expect trouble but be ready for anything."

The great bull looked at us and stopped in his tracks. His large trunk went up into the air and I knew he smelled us, even though we were down wind. He gave a blast from his trunk, with a loud sound that echoed like an avalanche. He started to charge at us and we had no place to go in the muddy flat open field. We readied our spears but they seemed such a puny defense against such a great beast.

Spotana leapt in front of the large

male, cutting off his charge and confusing him. The mammoth stopped, looked at the wolf, and shook his head from side to side. He looked at us, then back to the small wolf, unsure of what to do. His trunk went up and he gave another great blast then turned and continued to the South returning to his line of migration.

Suddenly, I remembered the story about my father, Loana, and the mammoth. The tale had become a campfire legend. How the wolf had saved him from the rogue mammoth. Was this the same bull? Spotana now joined her mother as part of the legend. It was good to have a wolf in the tribe.

108

Chapter 6

Spotana's Story

There was something unusual about the bull mammoth. I knew somehow that man and mammoths were not natural enemies. These big mammals were not hunters and were so big that they were usually safe from humans. Even a group of cave lions could not attack a herd of mammoths and neither could wolves. I knew instinctively that if I got his attention he would change his attack mode, possibly even calm down. After I charged, the bull looked confused but there was recognition in his eyes, as if he was remembering something that had happened before.

After the mammoths had passed, we continued to the cave. I went ahead and smelled the entrance, no large animal had taken refuge in it yet, but it was filled with rats. In I went in and they scattered. I chased them out but first caught a big one to share with my family.

My tribe arrived late in the day. The weather turned much colder and snow blew sideways making it hard to see. The people were cold and wet, but I smelled no frostbite in their muddy feet. They carried dry firewood. Surick rushed to the back of the cave and sparked a fire. It grew providing warmth. Curling up near the entrance, my favorite spot, I lay down and soon drifted off to sleep.

I dreamed I was part of a great wolf pack large enough to hunt rhinos and mammoths. Then the huge alpha-male turned on me, jumping on me and biting. I woke up with a yelp.

Jurick turned to me with a strange look and asked, "Are you alright, girl?"

I smacked my lips, curled up again and went back to sleep.

Restless Risana and I played often in the crowded cave. Jurick fed me every evening and brought me bones to chew. I made sure to relieve myself outside the cave even in the worst weather.

In the next month my belly started to

swell and my teats began to grow bigger. I was going to have puppies. I wondered how the tribe would deal with a group of young wolves. Would they accept them?

Winter continued to blow outside the cave and the snow piled higher than I could remember. One day I awoke with terrible cramps in my lower abdomen. I knew it was time for the puppies to come. I crawled to the small branch of the cave where I was born. Some instinct told me to push down on my belly. The pain was powerful when out came the first pup. I continued pushing with great pain in my loins. Gasping for air I pushed hard and out popped the second little pup. The process continued until five puppies were born. A wolf must be quiet while giving birth, so predators are not aroused. I followed this practice and kept silent even while in great pain. I quickly ate the afterbirth to keep the smell of birth from predators and to nourish myself enough to feed my pups.

I licked my brood, cleaning the tiny blind wolves. I loved them all immediately, sniffing each to distinguish their individual smell. Then I curled beside them and offered my offspring my belly. Each little pup found a place to feed. I panted and smiled. It had been a long hard night. So thirsty after the delivery, in the early morning while it was still dark, I carried each pup to the main part of the cave,

behind the fireplace and drank water from

the pool. Exhausted, I lay on my side, belly

exposed to the pups and I slept.

Chapter 7

Jurick's Story

I woke that morning to the sound of a storm outside and whimpering inside. The cave fire had almost gone out in the night but my focus went behind it. We knew Spotana was due to have puppies soon but I was amazed to see the five little wolves suckling on mother teats. I fed the fire a new log, then went to where my mother lay asleep. I shook her awake, excited.

"What is it, Jurick?" she asked me. She knew I wouldn't wake her up unless something important had happened.

"Spotana has had her puppies. She is in the back of the cave."

Silvana and I maneuvered back behind the fire where the five baby wolves suckled and whimpered. We took stock of them. Two were pure white, a male and a female, larger than the three other pups. The smallest female was spotted all over with brown on her face. The other two, a boy and a girl were almost like twins: black on the tips of their tails and dark streaks throughout their fur. Their faces were white but they had a black streak from their nose to their eyes. Spotana panted, lips curled in a smile, lying on her side to offer milk to her pups.

After taking stock, the tribe spent the day debating. That night the tribe met in council to decide what to do about the pups. Turick said, "We should kill these puppies. It is one thing to have one wolf with the tribe, but what will we do with a whole pack? Orick is dead and none of us can control Spotana like he did."

My mother took her turn, "It would not make Mother Nature happy to kill the puppies. They are not our prey. It is important that we do not harm them."

Surick, now our leader, decided for the tribe, "Let's see what happens as they get bigger. The puppies will be vulnerable for a long time."

Spotana's brood grew much faster than we expected. We had never seen how fast wolves matured. The puppies played, peed and pooped. I was responsible for cleaning up after the litter and tried to teach them to go outside the cave like Spotana. No one had ever watched a litter of pups interact before. It was obvious that the two white wolves were dominating the others. They could hold down the striped and spotted pups and keep them from mother's milk when they were hungry. Only mother wolf could control them to make sure the little ones were able to suckle.

As they grew bigger, the white pups often growled at me when I tried to control them. The smaller three would turn over in submission when I approached. We spent long hours together in the cave and in five months the young wolves were ready to wean from mother's milk yet the winter was still blasting outside the cave, so it was not yet time to teach them to hunt.

The puppies had learned to relieve themselves outside, trained by me and their mother. The white male was returning from relieving himself outside when my little sister Risana jumped on him to play. The young male wolf growled nastily and bit her on the arm and shoulder drawing blood. Surick quickly poked the young wolf with his spear. He yelped and retreated to the back of the cave with his mother.

My mother quickly comforted my

crying sister covering her wounds with herbs and hide, then wrapping the leather with twine.

She turned to Surick and said, "The two young white wolves are too wild to keep in the cave."

Turick said, "We should have killed the pups while they were little."

Silvana replied. "The three smaller wolves are not a threat. They are like how Spotana was when she was younger. We should let them stay."

Turick argued, "We can still kill them all. They can turn on us when we sleep.

Lurick consented. "I think we should

at least kill the two white wild ones now."

My mother, the spiritual leader of the tribe said "We owe it to Spotana not to kill them. I am a mother and would defend my young to death yet the wild white wolves cannot stay. We should drive them away."

Surick made a decision, "I agree. The two large white young wolves should go. Turick, get your spear. We will drive them away."

The two men went to the back of the cave and began to poke the larger white young wolves with their spears. The two growled and showed their teeth. Spotana retreated to the back of the cave with her three smaller youngsters. Two other men grabbed their spears and together drove the young wolves out of the cave into the cold, wet winter. The two white wolves stopped outside and snarled. The men threw rocks at them hitting the wolves until they trotted away with their tail between their legs..

Men were posted as guards to make sure the young wolves would not come back.

I hurried back to Spotana and the other young wolves. The youngsters rolled over in submission. I petted them in reassurance and they licked my arms and hands. Spotana sniffed at me and put her head against my leg.

"It's alright, girl." I said. She let me scratch her behind the ears. She seemed to understand that her two wild offspring had

to go away from the tribe.

Chapter 8

Spotana's Story

It was still icy cold when the tribe expelled my two young wolves. I went out each day to release my waste and in minutes I felt the savage bite of winter. It was an unusually long and difficult season. The snow was deep and the temperature dangerous. I knew the two wolves had to find food and shelter quickly. I remembered a small dug out in the rocks not far from the cave. I howled loudly to my two wild youngsters. Only the wind howled back. They were gone. Their aggressive nature would serve them well in the wild but even I knew they could not live with my human tribe. I took heart

seeing remnants of a fox skeleton. Almost

everything had been devoured I was sure

this was the work of my offspring. It gave

me some hope they would survive.

Chapter 9

Jurick's Story

The young wolf pups in the cave were full and warm. Without their two more aggressive brother and sister it was easier for them to get at mother's milk. The tribe's supplies were running low, but I would sneak dried pieces of meat for Spotana and her growing pups. It was still too cold outside for the mother wolf to wean the six-month-old puppies.

Spotana learned to hunt with my father. I wanted a wolf-hunting partner. There was something about the female striped pup that attracted me. After the first time I fed her from my hand, she would jump on me to play and lick my face. I noticed her jaw line was a little bit smaller than her mom's. The striped female would follow me all over the cave getting under my feet. I decided to give her a name. She had a black streak that ran from her nose to her eyes. Like the females in our tribe, her name should have ended in "-ana," but I named her Blacknose in spite of our tradition. The name caught on with the tribe and soon she came when I called her by name.

As winter eased its violence, Blacknose and I were always together in the cave. At night, she curled up next to me and we slept together sharing body warmth.

Surick decided to adopt the striped male wolf for his hunting partner. Surick taught the male pup to chase a bone like I did with Spotana. Surick named him Durick, a strong male name. No one had yet adopted the spotted female but we gave her the name Breana. We were amazed that all the young canines learned their names, together as part of our tribe.

Chapter 10

Spotana's Story

The tribe returned to the tundra and put up the huts. The journey had been more difficult because the heavy snows of winter turned the small streams into raging currents. Blacknose, Durick, and Breana refused to cross the first stream. Only after they watched me swim across the fast flowing stream and howl at them from the far bank would they thrust into the water. Wolves swim naturally but cold water goes right through our fur to the skin. We avoid the icy water when we can. When the pups got to the other side they looked skinny with wet fur. They shook the wet from their coats as they came out of the water.

The men and women desperately crossed each rapid flow, floating their skins, tools, and other possessions on branches, with the water sometimes coming up to their chests. The children took turns piggybacking on the backs of the men. Yet we all made it to the camp area safely. The flowing water pooled on the tundra making a lake in the center while new tall grass grew on each side. As usual in the spring, mud was everywhere.

The reindeer had not arrived yet and Surick, Jurick, the striped puppies, and I went to hunt for rabbits. We moved back toward the direction of the cave to seek our lost two brothers. Jurick found them first under a mound of fast melting snow. We circled around them, the two young white wolf carcasses perfectly preserved in their icy grave. I smelled the ground then urinated leaving my scent. Blacknose and Durick came over and urinated on their dead brother and sister, leaving their scent in tribute. The winter had been too cold for them. They would not see another.

Chapter 11

Jurick's Story

Spotana smelled them first, she growled and her offspring went on full alert. The reindeer were late arriving to the tundra. Probably the cold winter and deep snows slowing their migration. We grabbed our spears ready for predators or a raid from another tribe. Two men and a girl slowly approached our camp. We knew these people. They were from the tribe just to the South and had been seen often hunting on the tundra. There was a mutual respect between our tribes and we had traded tools with them before.

Their leader approached putting his

spear down to show he was coming in peace. Surick walked to him without his spear. The two men were distant cousins.

"Why do you come, Dunk?" Surick asked.

I listened closely to their conversation. Words sounded different in the mouths of the Southern tribe.

"We have seen your trained wolves on the hunting fields and we would like to know if you would trade one to our tribe." Dunk replied, looking carefully at the young canines.

Surick looked thoughtful for a minute, and then asked, "What would you like to offer?"

Dunk went back to a sled of branches and returned with a large wooly mammoth hide. "What an impressive blanket. How did you get it?" Surick asked.

Dunk quickly told the story. "An old mammoth female was sick and dying near our village. The other pachyderms of her group surrounded her and when she fell to the ground two bulls tried to help her, but she was too sick and could not get up. While the old mammoth lay dying, the rest of the herd would not leave her for two days and we did not get too close. Even after she died the other mammoths would not leave. Finally on the third day the herd moved on. We waited to make sure the others had left. In the late afternoon we moved in to dress down the dead female, taking the hide but leaving the meat of the dead sick animal. We knew it was bad luck to eat meat from something you did not kill."

Surick said, "I will meet with my tribe. I think we have a wolf pup for you. There is a young spotted wolf no one has claimed yet."

"Good," Dunk said, "but we have another proposition for you. You have a boy, Lurick, who is of age for a wife. We have a girl here, Jan, who has reached her twelfth birthday. She is ready for a mate."

Surick nodded. "This could be a

good match. Let them meet for a time in the hut of his family. If the two accept each other and the tribe agrees we could have a match."

"Her father is here, we could have the wedding feast tonight," Dunk said and the other foreigner stepped forward with his daughter. "This is Borg, the girl's father."

Surick and Borg bowed slightly to each other. The boy and the girl were led to the hut where they could talk to each other away from the tribe.

"Jurick, get these travelers some water and food," Surick said to me.

Our guests moved to look at the tame

136

wolf that they wanted in trade. The young couple moved shyly into the hut together.

A short time later Lurick and Jan had emerged from the hut together. They were holding hands. The tribe had agreed to trade the spotted puppy for the mammoth hide. I was smiling. That night there would be a marriage feast for my friend Lurick.

Jan looked beautiful that evening. A crown of wildflowers adorned her golden hair. She had been taken to a stream and immersed in the cold water to purify her body for mating.

The bride's name was changed to Jana so she could become part of our tribe. A huge pot of rabbit stew was prepared for

137

the feast. My mother placed a whole rabbit into the campfire as a sacrifice to Mother Nature and asked her to bless the marriage with children. The couple circled the fire ten times for luck, then retreated to a newly built hut constructed by the tribe for the newlyweds. The couple departed for their first night together and the rest of the tribe stayed up to sing songs around a blazing campfire while our wolves howled in harmony.

Chapter 12

Spotana's Story

The reindeer returned to the tundra and the high green grass around the new lake. The sun was shining and I felt its warmth. Fish were feeding on mosquitoes, causing circles to appear on the water's glimmering surface. I panted to cool myself and a smile came to my face.

My son and daughter had proven themselves naturals working with the tribe on hunting expeditions. We went off on another hunt and the three of us picked out a healthy deer, growling and snapping at it to separate it from the herd and chase it back towards the tribal hunters. Surick and

Lurick were waiting with the trip wire and when the big doe fell, the other men jumped in with their spears making short work and killing the deer. The men carried the kill back to the village and the women quickly started carving out the carcass.

"Spotana, Blacknose come here." Jurick said as he held two pieces of meat for my daughter and me. We responded with tails wagging and carefully taking the meat from the boy.

Surick called, "Durick! Come!" and gave him a large piece of meat.

We were happy and well fed with this tribe of men. I smelled the scent of wild wolves in the distance and looked up to see my relatives running after a deer, knowing they were now rivals, but regal predators. I also knew I would never run with those wild wolves again. I had a new family.

Epilogue

Alexei and Anastasia, two Russian college students, hiked off the main trail in the Mongolian foothills south of Irkutsk. Alexei tripped over a boulder and fell right into a bush. Cussing out loud, he looked to his side and saw a small hidden opening in the granite face.

"Anastasia, look at this! Help me move some rocks."

As the rocks were removed, the two young hikers realized they were at the mouth of a small cave. They entered and noticed light coming from an opening in the cave's roof. Alexei shined his flashlight on the cave wall.

"Anastasia, over here, look at this! Unbelievable." He stared at the cave wall.

The hikers were looking at a mural, faded but unmistakable, with primitive drawings of reindeers, wolves, human hunters, and even a large bear. They looked on in awe. They were tempted to tell their family and friends, but decided to keep the cave a secret until they returned to University at Saint Petersburg. When they arrived, Alexei and Anastasia ran across the campus. They had a favorite biology professor they wanted to share in the find.

The English sky was gray for a week.

The present weather report said "drizzle" to be followed by a long period of fog and rain. Dima Kuzlov Watson worked in her office in. Oxford at the University. She was a well-known anthropologist with a professorship at the renowned college. Dima was a modern international woman: born in Russia; she went to college in Paris, awarded a Masters in Saint Petersburg and a PhD at UC Berkeley in California. The woman spoke five languages fluently. Dr. Watson worked on digs on three continents, looking for and finding dinosaur fossils in Montana, bones of early man in Africa and priceless artifacts in China. Married to an Englishman, Dima had a daughter and the anthropologist had published three successful books and was known as one of the pre-eminent anthropologists in the world.

When the biology professor at Saint Petersburg explained the cave to Dr. Watson and asked for her help, she couldn't wait to start an expedition. The woman packed, kissed her little girl and husband goodbye, hugged the dog and boarded a British Air flight to Moscow. She arrived in the Russian capital, then was whisked off to the site in Mongolia.

Dima entered the cave with the biology professor. What she saw on the wall was truly amazing. It was a mural of art better preserved and more detailed than even the famous drawings at the Lascaux cave in Southern France. She explored the cave and the grounds for a week and found charred fossil bone just outside the cave. By summer, fifty-five students from Oxford, Berkeley and Russia were working at the dig led by the multilingual Professor Watson. Carbon dating showed the Ice Age people had lived there about 20,000 years ago.

As Dr. Watson looked up at the mural the pictures jumped out at her and filled her mind with a story. She immediately sat down and outlined the story of ice age wolves and a tribe of people. She could see the wolves hunting with the cave men and women, working together to find shelter from the cold, icy landscape. She knew she had to write the story of the mural.

Dima was wakened out of her dream by Joseph, an American graduate student.

"Professor, I think you want to see this."

A jawbone had been carefully excavated out of the ground. She examined it carefully and decided to take it back to a mammal-biologist in Moscow to be sure. The results were startling. The mammal expert looked at her with a big smile on his face.

"I think you better alert the Nobel Prize Committee. The jawbone is a cross between a wolf and a dog."

Dima carefully took the bone in her gloved hand, looking at it deep in thought and aware of its unique significance. She realized she had another piece of the puzzle to add to her story and to her scientific resume. She smiled and thought of her Labrador retriever at home with her husband and daughter. She missed her family - her tribe -all three of them.

Author's Note

This book is a work of fiction. All characters are fictional.

My inspiration for this story comes from an ABC News Program in 2001on the genetic origins of dogs. Modern DNA testing shows that all modern dogs evolved from wolves. The period of the domestication of the first wolves is highly disputed, from 30,000 to 14,000 years ago. The latest research concerning the location of the transition is also in dispute but Asia is believed to be the best candidate. This is why I changed the location of the anthropological research on the cave in this second edition of the book from France to Mongolia.

Most biologists believed that the evolution from wolves to dog came slowly over hundreds of years. That hypothesis changed after a study of farm foxes by Russian scientist Dmitry Belyaev. It showed that if "people-friendly" silver foxes were carefully bred, their genetic code changed to be more dog-like, resembling border collies, in just nine generations. We now have the hypothesis that wolf domestication came about just as quickly because early man bred people-friendly dogs. The wolves that "*found shelter from the cold*" became friends with man and the two species that began as rivals ended in an amazing symbiosis.

Made in the USA
Charleston, SC
24 February 2013